T0077991

A Collection of Tales

CHICK GALLIN

ARCHWAY
PUBLISHING

This is a work of fiction. All of the characters, names, incidents, organizations, and dialogue in this novel are either the products of the author's imagination or are used fictitiously.

Archway Publishing books may be ordered through booksellers or by contacting:

Archway Publishing
1663 Liberty Drive
Bloomington, IN 47403
www.archwaypublishing.com
844-669-3957

Because of the dynamic nature of the Internet, any web addresses or links contained in this book may have changed since publication and may no longer be valid. The views expressed in this work are solely those of the author and do not necessarily reflect the views of the publisher, and the publisher hereby disclaims any responsibility for them.

Any people depicted in stock imagery provided by Getty Images are models, and such images are being used for illustrative purposes only. Certain stock imagery © Getty Images.

ISBN: 978-1-6657-1306-1 (sc)
ISBN: 978-1-6657-1307-8 (e)

Library of Congress Control Number: 2021919927

Print information available on the last page.

Archway Publishing rev. date: 4/29/2022

in memorium to my
late wife Linda

A Tennis Tale

I n the world of tennis there are three very distinct categories, rankings, if you must be clear.

The Beginner, whose efforts leave very much to be desired. As a beginner you have no "strokes" nor any appreciable "style." The only thing you have as a beginner is a sense of … hope …

The Intermediate, where your strokes, style and hopes are starting to surface into some semblance of form.

Next, are the Advanced players, that is the ranking when all three facets of the game come together and you play a very decent game of tennis, with a good deal of satisfaction and or pain, because pain is a very integral part of any sport that you engage in.

I am the penultimate Intermediate player, whose ranking fall between a 3.0 and 3.5 with no discernible degree of proficiency . In other words I am a hacker. My tennis game is not so much a "game" but a constant battle with myself, my racket, the ball and lastly my opponent. To say that I have not the most consistent type of game would not in the least bit of exaggeration but the honest truth.

There are times (mostly all the time) when my hands and feet are working totally against each other. In a game where hand, feet and eye have to work in concert with each other I fail miserably. I also cannot seem to find the right racket for me. They are either too light or too heavy or the strings are either too loose or too tight. In other words, I am a mess as a tennis player.

I have struggled for many years, trying to gain some semblance of craftsmanship of this game, but as of this moment I remain just another … Hacker …

Now, from time to time our Pro-shop features rackets from different companies who hope to sell these rackets to the players at the club. I have tried in vain, to find a racket from one of these companies that one of them might help to change my game and give me a little sense of something happening to my mediocre game, but until now nothing has worked.

Well, I was playing (battling) one day when to my complete surprise, I broke a string. I have often heard of the advanced players breaking strings quite often. They hit the ball with a lot of power, something I have not mastered, in all my years of playing. So when I broke the string I was almost ecstatic thinking "Wow I must have hit the ball really hard." I was patting myself on the back until I looked at my racket and saw that I had only worn down the strings until they were really thin.

But now, I had no racket to play with and my partner said I should go to the Pro-shop and ask for a loaner, so I could finish my match.

The Pro-shop manager, knowing me and my game, said I couldn't have one of the newer rackets, but I could find a used racket that they keep for this situation . I hefted three or four rackets which didn't feel quite right, I kept trying until I found one that felt O.K. The racket needed a new grip and the frame was chipped in a few places, but I figured it would do for the time I needed it for. So, I took it and went back to my game.

From the start I could feel something different . I didn't know if it was something about me or something in the air, but there was a definite difference. I felt a stirring in my body, a sort of springiness in my legs and as I waited to return the next serve I knew I was going to hit the ball just right. The ball came to me and without conscious thought I slammed the ball with a stroke I did not know I possessed. The ball went sharply down the middle of the court to one inch of the baseline for a winner. I couldn't believe it. It was as if someone else had hit that ball. I looked at the racket in amazement, wondering what I did, and lined up on the court as my partner awaited to return his serve, which he promptly hit into the net.

It was my turn again to receive serve and I just as promptly hit a stinging angle shot that caught my opponent completely off guard. We won that game and as the match went on, with me doing everything right, my partner and I won the match easily. I could not believe what had happened.

My partner and our opponents praised the way I had played and I was in seventh heaven. The racket had to be returned and as I entered the Pro-shop the manager said, "Your racket is ready, we restrung it while you were playing."

I was reluctant to return the loaner but as I did something seemed to leave my body, I had a distinct feeling of loss that was something I could not figure out. I went home knowing something different had happened to me and I wondered what it was.

Going back to the tennis courts two days later, I hoped that what I had done the other day was not a fluke, that my game had suddenly turned a corner and I could move up to better games.

Unfortunately, this was not to be. The same foursome awaited me and as the game started I fell back into my same inconsistent routine. I no longer seemed to be able to hit stinging returns, my serve was again mediocre, and I floundered on the court as I had in the past. The magic was gone and we were beaten handily by other mediocre players. No surprise, I was disappointed and feeling that I had let my partner down. I walked away from the courts very depressed.

Some days later I returned to the courts, and as I prepared to play I went to get my racket out of my tennis bag. It was supposed to be there, I know I put it there after playing the other day, but it was not there. There was not any other place it could be, I couldn't imagine where it was.

"Come on" insisted my partner and our opponents.

"I lost my racket" I replied, "I'll have to get a loaner". I ran to the Pro-shop and asked for the loan of a racket, hoping the same racket I had used the other day was still available. It was and I trotted back out to the court.

"I'm ready, let's play" I said.

The same feeling came over me as it did the other day, and I was looking forward to the game as I have never done before. Needless to say, as anxious as I was to see myself play well was overshadowed by a feeling that this might be another mediocre day for me. But it not to be, I played out of my mind, making shots that in my life and my wildest dreams I could never imagine I could make. It was amazing, I played with style, daring and accuracy. We trounced the other team, even though my partner was still the player he always was. This was no reflection on him, because before today, so was I .Feeling as I was I couldn't wait to get to the Pro-shop to start negotiating to buy the racket. It cost much more than the racket was worth, but just had to have it. For me it was a steal.

I couldn't wait to play again, I knew there was something about the racket that had an extreme effect on me and I didn't waste time trying to figure it out. But I couldn't just take it on faith, I still wondered,"What's going on ',I asked myself," What should I do ?"

Without thinking I went up to one of the better players and asked if he would play a set with me . He looked at me and said, " You want me to play with you ?"

I said a bit sheepishly, " Yes, I would like to see how I would do against you, ".I said a bit sheepishly."

Okay, but only one set," he said.

It was a strange sight to see, me the hacker and him the accomplished player . But onward and upward I thought to myself, what could happen . He could wipe up the courts with me or I might surprise myself and take a game or two from him … no big deal.

But it was a big deal to me, I shook a little at first, I wasn't really a singles player and a reputed hacker to boot. But stranger things have happened .

He hit a blazing serve to me while I was still wondering what had possessed me to do this with a player of his caliber, anyway, the serve went passed me like a shot, I made no move to even return it . The next serve was just as fast but this time I was prepared, I took it as it bounced high and I hit a solid shot down the middle of the court that hit the tape at the service line and bounced over his head for my point.

The rest of the set went back and forth in scores until I had him40-Love on my serve. With one more point in the set in my favor I reared back and with all of my strength I hit my serve. It was then I heard the most devastating sound I could hear … ping … I broke a string, his return was right to my forehand which I had been blasting the whole set. But now, with no tension in my strings I shanked the ball into the net . With no other racket to play with I conceded the set to him.

"You played an unbelievable set my friend, you had me until your strings broke, you have turned into a terrific player "he said to me, "We will have to do this again sometime, thanks for the game."

"Great, thanks for giving me a chance, I look forward to the next time." I said.

I walked back to the Pro-shop to have my racket strung and said I would like to pick it up in a day or two.

By the next time I was scheduled to play I had dreams of my playing with all the good players at the courts, thinking that my new found progress had been noticed by everyone . I still had my regular game though and I walked out on the court with my newly strung racket, full of confidence.

Warming up did not give me the same feeling as I had the other day, but I still felt confident . I still felt I could perform better than my opponents, until my opponents first serve, which was no way near the serves of the other day which I had destroyed. I hit the ball with my forehand and it flew backward into the fence behind me.

The rest of the match was a fiasco for me. There was

nothing resembling the 'new me' I had been the other day. I felt nothing that I had felt and did nothing that was worthy of anything but a mediocre player that I had returned to.

My questions are," Was it the racket with the old strings, was that the magic that had transformed me, or was it something that happened to me that was fleeting, never to return. Or was it all a ... Dream ..."?

The End.

The Male Mystique
Illusions & Delusions

Charlie was listening, with a wistful, rapt look on his face, as Benny recounted his escapade of the previous night .

"So there I am with this fantastic looking blond that I met at the Palace bar. I mean to tell you, she was an absolute dream . Nothing about this chick was negative, I mean, the face, the figure, the attitude was class A, and pulsating . What I'm saying gentlemen, what I am saying is, all I had to do is touch her and she " came ", that's how primed she was. So after a drink or two I suggested we move out of the joint and get someplace less noisy and less crowded, and right away she pipes up "let's go to my place ". Man !!! Just like that ... It was perfect, off we go, and in the car she was just as hot to trot as she was in the bar . She kept running her hand up and down my thigh, mostly up, with her other hand she was doing things under her dress that I couldn't see but could only imagine, and man it kept her motor running .

Well, we get to her place and I couldn't get out of the car fast enough for her . She was at her door with the key in the lock and turning it like it was too hot to touch. I didn't even get a chance to look around her place when she grabbed me and was all over me, tearing at my clothes, dragging me into the bedroom . Man, oh, man, I couldn't wait and obviously she couldn't either .

O K ... here we are going at it, hot and heavy, boy, was she hot ... She's all lathered up and moving, and I am working away like a jackhammer, I'm making her moan and groan and bite, oh how she could bite, God I was driving her crazy .

All of a sudden, I'm just about to pop, and she lets out a sound, like an animal, and just like a giant vise she clamps on me and, bang, I 'm shooting my wad like crazy, oh what a feeling ... oh wow, she went bananas when she felt that and she goes wild under me . She starts yelling ' Oh God, Oh Jesus '.

Give it to me, I can't stand it anymore Ohhh ---Benny you're driving me crazy !!!

I tell you I shot my wad so hard it bounced off the walls of her snatch, and it just drove her crazy .

She went on like that for three or four more minutes, squirming and moaning, kissing my neck and face and cry-ing real tears. Charlie, oh man, I made her come like she never came before, and did she love it . Oh man I came all over her insides like she never had it before . Wow !!! She sure was a hot numberf, and I really gave it to her good, Charley, I really put out her fire … Oh man!!

You have probably heard conversations like that before, and I guess guys, you really believe all that stuff because you like to live vicariously through someone else 's fantasies . But have you ever bothered to ask a woman exactly what she really feels during sex, I doubt it and I doubt whether she will not want to risk hurting your feelings . Well I finally asked, and guys I think you ought to sit down for this.

Don't bank on the idea that you were the only reason the 'chicks' were moaning, groaning, biting and screaming . With a greater part of the female population the clitoral stimulation of just body parts and pubic hair is the reason for it all . The amount of stimulation you provide with your penis has very little to do with the act and if you think you drove them crazy with your ejaculation, coming shooting or whatever you like to call it … don't count on it .

Many women scarcely feel you inside them, what with natural lubrication and all, and guys, we are not all as big as we think we are, but you keep on believing, cause what else have we got to cling to but that . Let's face it dildo's and vibrators achieve the same results as we do, if not better.

Anyway, back to basics, all the magazines and paperback books picture women as going crazy for the stud … women as I am now led to believe are just as satisfied with a sensitive guy as a lover, as much as a 'macho man 'who believes he is the Rock of Gibraltar '. O K back to your shooting sky rockets and hitting the walls of her insides, the amount of semen secreted in ejaculation may just about fill a thimble and as for the force of ejaculation it falls way short of the walls and is rarely felt by the lady if ever . Actually, the only time she would know you came would be during oral sex and that would only occur if she was awake ...

So, I'm sorry guys, I know your 'male egos ' insist on the idea that you have loaded cannons,ready for battle, your cannons are loaded alright, but with wad cutters . We still would like to go around with the idea that we are like cavemen and our sexual encounters and conquests are subjected to our blasting right through her back, but it just ain't so ...

So, Ladies, please, keep up our illusions, even if they are only delusions ... we need it .

The End.

Changes

The city was quiet, and glistened after a quick shower washed across the sky giving the streets and lawns a pearlized appearance. The air cooled briefly, but returned to its former humidity almost at once. The air was still and the scent of the freshly dampened grass was pleasant in my nostrils. I was headed for the bank to get some cash from the ATM, as I needed some for the morning and couldn't take the time before work.

Passing the shopping center, which had already been closed for several hours, I really didn't give any thought to the time. I had so many things on my mind and paid no attention to what was or was passing or happening around me. To say I was practically unconscious to my surroundings would be understatement.

I pulled up to the curb of the bank's ATM window and

leaving my car running, I walked up to and confronted man's natural enemy, the computer. Again I was absorbed in my own problems, and also attempting to conquer the teller machines instructions. All I needed was fifty dollars, and it finally came sliding from the slot like so much worthless paper from between the lips of the machine. I collected the bills and was waiting for my card to be returned to me as I hummed a senseless tune, until I was brought up short by a sharp object being pressed into the small of my back. An accented voice whispered gratingly in my ear "I'm going to take your money, my friend, don't try anything stupid or you are going to get hurt, comprendo?" I froze with the shock of the object in my back, and the threat that put my mind into deep freeze. "I only have fifty dollars", I said, "you can have it all,"

My mind started racing just about then, trying to formulate a plan of action, something that might get me past this point of numb inaction.

"Don't make any moves that will get you killed, another voice boomed in the still night air. This came from my other side and as I swung my head in reaction, I saw a black shadow moving to my left and out of my line of vision. Still, I could feel him move up closer, cutting off a move to that side. At the time I couldn't, and didn't realize he had done me a great favor in preventing my natural reflexes from a foolish move. I stood quietly, not wanting to put myself in a more dangerous position.

"Give me your card, and no funny stuff, or I'll have him carve you up like a leg of mutton, you hear, now give me that card, and be careful, I mean it" he said with a coldness in his voice that made a chill run up my spine. I could think of nothing else to do but comply. I did as I was told. I took out my wallet and handed it over. He took out my card and as he did I stepped back a pace. It was then that I got a look at the two men that had me in their power. The one who had the knife in my back was about five foot eight and one hundred sixty five pounds, dark and wiry, with a three day growth of stubble on his face that looked like it could only be removed with a blow torch. His eyes were like back dots and he squinted in the dark like a snake about to strike. His hand held a ten inch spring loaded switchblade which glinted in the light from the street lamp on the corner. He handled it like it was a sex object in a mind in which phallic symbols were represented by instruments of pain and torture. He smiled, an oily dark smile which ran across his face like sludge from a leaking engine, "You are pussy, man" he growled, "No balls". I had to agree with him for the time being, anyhow. The other guy was about six feet two and two hundred twenty five pounds, encased in a muscular frame. I weighed out at one hundred ninety pounds and was in fairly good shape. By this time he was at the ATM window trying to get the machine to feed him money, apparently with little success as he roared at the window. He suddenly slammed his big meaty fist into the window shaking the frame into a rattling, blurry blankness. No lights were visible in the window, and as he turned I could see poison in his eyes.

"Godammit, get your ass over here and get this thing to work, now ..." he bellowed, shaking with rage.

Ignoring his command, I gathered my wits about me, trying to assess my options with these two. I knew I would not have many chances, if any, but I knew I would have to try. It wasn't the money, they could take that, with my blessings. It was the way they were taking me for a wimp, just because I didn't resist right away.

The next few moments would tell whether my life meant anything or my rears of training in martial arts were for nothing.

"I said get your lily white fucking ass over here and get us some more money, boy, and I mean right now ..." he hissed with the side of his face all screwed up and getting uglier than it was before, and it was ugly before, believe me.

"Godammit, I said now ..." he roared again.

I took one step toward the window and as I did my right hand came up from my side, and with an upward chopping motion I caught the knife holder under his nose, forcing the nostrils and cartilage upwards into his eye sockets, causing him to drop his knife and bring both his hands to his face in excruciating pain. He tried unsuccessfully to push all that mess back to where it belonged, and only succeeded in causing even more damage to his already broken nose. There was blood and mucus membrane gushing from the center of his face and I figured I could count him out of the picture for the time being.

In this one moment I had reduced my enemy to only one and was advancing on him with the element of surprise, at least, on my side. For the moment he was off guard, but, only for an instant his reflexes were quick, he rushed me as I was moving towards him, we almost collided, until the last milli-second. He side stepped and caught me with a side kick to my right calf. The pain registered and I fell away to the side and almost went down to the concrete sidewalk.

I swore, "Dammit," I cursed myself letting him catch me off guard like that. The only good that came of this lapse was the fact that I spied the switchblade and grabbed it as I came up off the ground. I held it behind my back as I circled the black man, who was unbuttoning his jacket. Moving towards me he brought out a black object, which didn't appear to be a gun, but looked menacingly like a bludgeon with a heavy ball if steel on its business end.

"Why you muthafucker, I'm going to have to hurt you real bad now, I told you not to try anything and you had to fuck up, didn't you?" he yelled and as he did he smiled as if he was going to enjoy himself, in fact he said, "I'm going to enjoy this ... you muthafucker."

I let him go on, and as he did I looked directly into his eyes it was like looking into a furnace with blazing hot coals, sparks seemed to shoot off in different directions. Using his eyes as a gauge I kept mine as cool as I could under the circumstances, letting him know that I was not going to turn over as easily as he thought I would, just because he was black and bigger than me and that he had a rather large and menacingly bad weapon, but who said I was smart. I let him move within a few steps of me when I sidestepped and jumped over his downed partner to give myself a little extra working room.

Strange noises began to come from the guy, not speaking noises but guttural sounds, like from an animal, an animal that I needed to take out of my world if I was to survive. I didn't doubt my ability to do this but I was dealing with an unknown quality in him. He still didn't know I now had the knife which I held behind me, in a position to either to bring it up or across. I didn't want to use it and I hoped I could make him back off before it became necessary.

It was now my turn to hiss through my teeth, "Make it easy on yourself, brother, you can take off now and save yourself a lot of pain and trouble. Your friend is not going to be any use to you for a long time coming, and you got nowhere to go if you don't leave now and take him with you," I said, "There's a lot more hurting in store for you if you want to keep on coming, but my advice is to split ... now."

"Man, you must be crazy if you think I'm goin to let you get away with this shit, I'm goin to bust yo head wide open and split is what I'm going to do to you, you ain't goin to need no doctor when I'm through with you, all you goin to need is the coroner, sucker," he boomed out in the still night sounding like a cannon exploding in an empty room. "I'm telling you to chill out man, or else, and get over here to this window and get me some cash … pronto … you dig," he growled.

Somehow I sensed a new tone in his voice, from one minute to the next he had changed and I couldn't figure it out, but it lent me a little hope. He suddenly lost the edge he had when he first exploded into my world, and I sensed he was looking for a little room to get himself off the hook he now found himself on. I guess he was expecting an older and less combative person, either an old man or a woman. I didn't want to let go of that sense and I advanced slowly on him, hoping to either throw him completely on unsteady ground or better yet make him believe I could hurt him in other ways besides physically.

"Give it up pal," I said, "You got yourself in deep shit with this one, I can pin all the teller robberies on you with this assault, with intent to kill, thrown in to boot. Give it up now or I can't guarantee you'll be treated kindly by the cops,". I hoped it sounded strong enough to put a little doubt in his mind, but I couldn't tell by his face which radiated a fierce hatred, and from his voice, which did little to convince me that he was giving up just yet.

"You shit, I told you to get over here and get me some cash, I don't give a shit about anything else, now you get yo ass over here now …", he roared.

"Well I warned you, I guess you like to live dangerously, not my problem anymore, so ... whatever you get you deserve," I said, with as much bravado as I could muster. I brought the switchblade around slowly so I would be ready when and if I needed it, and let him see it and think about it.

Just then a pair of headlights came around the corner of the bank and froze us both in our respective positions, he with his bludgeon and me with the switchblade.

Suddenly, he moved with the speed of a panther, he ran past me towards the driver's side of my car, my car ... with the keys in the ignition.

"No!!!, I yelled, and whirling around, I leapt over the form of his downed partner, and threw myself over the hood of the car, rolling as gracefully as I could, but as I tumbled over the hood my head knocked against the windshield. I saw stars and a myriad of colored lights, as I was trying to clear my head and at the same time trying to stop him, I made a desperate grab for his leg, hoping to at least to slow him down until help came. He had other ideas, I think, because, he swung his club down on my arm, it was like someone was tearing my arm off at the shoulder, and I bit down on my lower lip to keep from screaming with the pain. He had trouble opening the car door, and I had that moment to gather myself together and make a last 'stab' at him.

Stab was the right term, I swiped the knife out and caught him high on the thigh, he grunted but kept pulling at the door handle, gasping with the effort and the pain.

He gasped out, "Motherfucker, open up, dammit."

Now I had time, just a brief second, to pull myself up the side of the car, and with my left arm hanging and getting numb fast, I came after him again. This time I put the switchblade in front of his face and icily said, "It's now or never man, give it up."

"Shit on you man," he said, "I'm getting out of here, through you or any other way I can, so get out of my face motherfucker or I'm going to kill you." His eyes closed to slits, and I felt him about to move again, but this time I was ready for him, I thought. He swung his bludgeon straight out, and I backed up just enough to let it go past my face, I felt a rush of air from its passage and thanked whatever gods were in my corner at the time.

I didn't see him follow it up with a chop to my neck but my shoulder deflected it enough and I slashed away at his hand and caught the back of it deep enough to cause him to scream out in pain and drop the club. Blood was spurting everywhere, I must have cut an artery, he roared, and I knew he was at his most dangerous, he was cut on his hand and leg and was wild with pain and humiliation.

I backed away now, just to have a wider area to assess his next move, it came slowly, as if in a slow motion movie sequence. He charged with his arms out wide, like a bear, in full attack. I backed away a little more and suddenly I was falling backwards, the knife flying out of my hands and out of sight in the bushes behind me, I kept rolling backwards to at least put some distance between us, but he kept coming, roaring at the top of his lungs. It was a terrifying sound to hear coming from a human being, but at this time he was less than human.

"Hey, help me, for god's sake, do something," I yelled out to someone who had pulled up in a car, "Come on, before it's too late, let's go, help me."

Nothing happened, and the black storm kept coming. I finally gained some footing, but he barreled into me knocking me down again. This time he groped for my neck with hands that were like meat hooks, covered with blood. I pounded his face several times only to make him more determined to strangle the life out of me.

At any other time it is easy to discuss the merits of fighting fairly, but when your life hangs in the balance there doesn't seem to be any room for fairness, and this was one of those times. Those times were in another time and place, so I attacked his hands which were attached to my neck in a seemingly permanent position, his thumbs pressing against my windpipe. Gasping I reached for the hand with the knife wound and dug my fingers into the opening which was slippery with blood and sweat.

He roared again, but I kept up the pressure, ripping at his hand, hoping he would give in before I gave out. Little spots were appearing in front of my eyes and my breathing was becoming difficult. I didn't think I could hold on much longer and I kept thinking someone was enjoying this scene, otherwise they would have done something by now. I knew I was not enjoying this one little bit. My head was hurting more and more and my attempts to rip his hands became more feeble with every passing second. Blackness started to surround me and my hands started slipping from his.

"Hey, mister, are you ok, please open your eyes, please I don't know how long he will be out," someone said, it sounded female, young and scared.

Light came slowly to my eyes, and I choked once, wondering what had happened and why I was still alive, grateful, but wondering.

"Wha!!! what happened? Where is he?" I mumbled, raising myself with some difficulty, and shaking my head to clear it. I saw a huge form crumpled on the street, already stirring and groaning.

"Help me up, hurry, we don't have any time to waste," I ordered, and a soft female hand tried to pull me to my feet, without success, I had to do it myself. I rolled onto my knees and pushed as hard as I could in the weakened condition I was in, and slowly rose unsteadily to my feet. "Quick, get me that club over there" I indicated the bludgeon lying at the curb where he had dropped it when I slashed his hand.

As she rushed over to pick up the club, he was getting to his knees, shaking his head, like an animal who has lost a mighty battle.

"Ooohhh," he moaned, "what hit me?"

That's what I wondered about, and as I stood over him I said "If you want some more I can provide it, so you'd better stay down where you are." I showed him the club, and he rocked back on his heels, a gash showing over his right eye, flowing blood into his eye.

"Okay, man, I won't give you no more problems, just don't hit me no more," he groaned.

Still wary I shifted my position, until I could see him and my rescuer, I didn't want to give him any leeway. What I saw was a surprise and a shock. Before me was a young girl, possibly seventeen or eighteen years old, in jeans, a sweater and in her hand a rather large forty five caliber pistol, pointed in my direction, the barrel looking like the entrance to the Holland Tunnel.

"Say I'm glad you came along, and I'm glad you didn't use that on him. You stopped him well enough without it. ... could you point it a little bit over that way?" I pointed away from me and smiled, a smile that I didn't quite feel. What I did feel was a rush of anxiety, thinking to myself, "What the hell am I into now."

"You didn't think I helped you out of the goodness of my heart, did you?" she said and smiled, "If you did, you must think I'm stupid, or else you hit your head harder than I thought you did. I want your wallet and his, and I need you to drop that club ... over there ... where it can't hurt anybody." She pointed several yards away from me, and her.

I couldn't figure out why she helped me, and then this turnaround.

"What's going on? I don't get it, come on now, you don't want to do this." I looked into her eyes, they showed no emotion or feeling.. "This doesn't figure miss, you don't look like a crook … you helped me, you could have taken my wallet and his when we both were out … what's up?"

I continued to search her eyes for something, anything resembling sense, but, there was nothing. She could have taken what jewelry we both had, but she didn't, it just didn't figure.

"What you don't get is," she said coldly, "Any more help from me until you give me your wallet, and you've got just about five seconds to do that, before I get real nervous with this gun, do you understand that?"

I nodded, and said, "I understand, but all I have in my wallet is the fifty he tried to get, and he was as unsuccessful as you're going to be, not that I value the money, it's just I don't like to be pushed or ordered around … by anyone. So knowing that … where do we go from here. Pretty soon," I continued, "He is going to be up and around and you will have the two of us to contend with. It's your choice, sweetheart, him or me."

"Well, if I kill you both I won't have to make that choice, will I?" she retorted, "Now hand it over, sweetheart."

"Somehow I don't think you're going to use that thing on me. You had your chance and you didn't, and I don't think you'll do it now," I said, with a confidence I didn't necessarily feel. "Come on use your head, let's do this the easy way, and the smart way. I promise I won't turn you in, but for god's sake, we've got to do something about him and his friend over there, I did bloody them up somewhat."

"I don't care how bloody they are, or about you either," she said, and I believed her. "I just want your money and I'll get out of here, come on … your money … or else."

"Ok, ok, but I think you and I could do each other a lot better if we work together. You're a good looking girl, when you're not pointing a forty five at me, and I'm in the business of helping good looking girls," I lied, "I could get you into something more profitable, and less dangerous." I shut up then, hoping I hadn't overplayed my hand, giving her time to mull it over.

She didn't take more than a half of a beat when she said," Look, smart ass, I don't need your help so cut the bullshit and lay your wallet on the hood of the car and back off."

She had a good five step move to the car, I figured I could take her in that time. The only thing that worried me was the rock steady hold she had on the gun, which was no light-weight, but she did not, waver one bit. It convinced me that she knew how to handle it with no problem. I laid my wallet on the hood and said, "Here it is, you've got what you wanted, but I don't think it's going to do you much good," and as I said that I glanced over her shoulder, behind her.

She took the bait and turned slightly, no one was there of

course and when she turned back angrily neither was I. I threw myself over the hedge to her right and rolled to a standing position beside her. I reached out and grabbed the gun from her hand before she knew what was happening and pushed her out in front of me.

"So now what have we got here, three of you, all cut from the same pattern, beautiful, the only thing I can't figure out is what to do with you all. I guess I could shoot all of you and take off, I don't think anyone cares about three dead rip off artists, what do you think?" I asked her.

I expected her to beg and plead to be let go, and was disappointed when she didn't. She just stood there, as if it didn't matter to her what I did.

"Well, what's it going to be honey, you act as if you don't care, what's up? If you don't mind my asking."

"You're right, I really don't care or give a damn what you do, if you want to shoot, go ahead, if you want to turn me over to the cops ... do it ... just do it and let me be, I don't care."

"Come on, I meant what I said before," I said, trying to get her to open up a little, her attitude had thrown me, and I couldn't let it go. "I might be able to get you into something besides armed robbery, tell me you're not interested, just a little bit."

"Look, I don't want to bust your bubble pal, you want to be a good guy, try it on him," she motioned to the big black guy, "See if he's buying your line of crap today, or just either shit or get off the pot … shoot me or turn me in … or let me go, I don't need nor want your lectures, get it."

"Oh sure, you're a hard case, you are," I taunted, "Shoot me or send me up, that's great, oh yeah, what you don't realize is that I can tie you into these two sleaze balls, and make it stick. Would you like that? Or do you think that going straight is so tough that you can't hack it. Let me clue you in, sweetheart, you could make in the straight world, you've got guts and looks, you might be a little light in the brain department, from what I see here, but that's easy to overcome. You're not so tough or you would have cold cocked me like you did him it, would have been easy, but you didn't … why, or you could have waited and let him finish me and then taken care of him, again I ask, why?"

"I don't need this bullshit, pal," she spat out at me, what the hell are you anyway, a shrink? One minute you come off like a cop and the next minute your analyzing me, get off of it will you, and don't tell me about your straight life … it stinks. I was straight a lotta years and what have I got to show for it … nothing … so take your looks, guts, and brain theory and stick it."

I had wanted to get her blood up, and I did, and if she would have had something to hit me with she would have and loved it, so I changed tactics.

"Put your pocketbook down, in front of you and back off, over there and around that mail box. Keep your hands on top of the box."

When she had done this I picked up her bag and looked at her I.D. credit cards, driver's license and all the little things women find to stuff in their bags, but no money.

"Silvia Grey, that's your name ... eh ... or did you steal all this I.D.," I asked and got no answer, she just looked at me, with a tight look around her eyes. The picture on her license matched, so I guessed she didn't need to answer.

I threw her bag back to her and told her to hug the mailbox like it was her last hold on the world. I didn't need her coming at me right now.

I walked cautiously to the black guy, who was coming around slowly and reached into his back pocket. I grabbed his wallet and stepped back out of range and positioned myself so that they were both in front of me and well away.

Harlan Stafford, the driver's license read and the picture proved it was him. I kept his license and tossed his wallet back to him, hitting his head with it, "Uhnnn," he groaned as he sat on the ground holding his head in his hands, looking dazedly around at the situation. I guess he didn't like what he saw, because he uttered a loud "Shit man."

"Harlan", I said, "This chick went upside your head, and now you are both mine. The question is, what do I do with you? Maybe you have an idea ... come on ... try something out on us and see if we can come up with a solution."

He looked at me with a funny look on his face, and then looked over at Sylvia, then back at me, "What the fuck is going on here man? Just who the fuck are you man? I never run into this kind of shit before, what do you want man "You gotta want something from us", he snarled. "What you gonna do with that gun man? And don't be pointing it at me that way."

It would have been funny, if it wasn't so serious. Me, standing with a gun, trained on a black hood, and a white female crook, and a Latin male rip off artist with a bloody face, what a picture. I wasn't sure what I wanted to do, I really couldn't figure it out.

It turned out that I didn't have to. Just then a car came wheeling around the hedge, headlights blinding, brakes squealing, right into the middle of the four of us. The dust that was kicked up resembled a dust storm in the desert.

Immediately I was up on my feet, the forty five held out in front of me in a two handed grip. I was blinded by the head lights and the dust, and I screamed out, "Turn off those head lights, dammit." I couldn't see a thing for several moments, and when I heard the car door open I pointed the gun in that direction.

"Don't shoot, don't shoot, please!!!" yelled out a male voice as the dust settled around the area.

"Stay where you are," I hollered, and quickly looked around. It was as if nothing had ever happened. There was no Sylvia Grey … no Harlan Stafford … no bleeding Latino … it was just me, and the new intruder and our cars. I stared at the spot where Harlan had been, and shook my head, as much to clear it as to try and understand what had gone on here. It fleetingly crossed my mind that maybe this was a dream, but my head and useless arm denied that.

"What the hell is going on here? Hey you … what the hell is going on here … I said," the figure behind the car door yelled out at me.

I never realized that the forty-five had pulled my arm down by its sheer weight, and I was standing there with my shoulders sagging, in a crouched position, with a confused look on my face.

"Godammit, I said what the hell is going on here? Hey man are you alright? What's this all about?" He repeated, as if I owed him an explanation.

"Nothing's going on here, absolutely nothing," I said, and slowly drove out of the parking lot and went home.

"Well, I thought to myself it's getting tougher all the time to borrow a couple of bucks."

The moon shone just as bright as before, and the grass still sparkled from the rain and I figured no one would ever believe it if I told them.

"Nothing really ever changes after all, does it?"

The End.

The Pack

The night wasn't especially dark, as a matter of fact there was a brilliant moon and the visibility was great.

I had left my friends at the end of the party and decided to walk the half mile to the taxi stand rather than getting a lift from one of them. As I said the night was brilliantly moonlit and it seemed a good idea at the time.

But now ... well ... it did seem like a good idea.

I felt their presence before I actually heard them. They moved sporadically, as if one was covering the other, sure of their moves. When one was in place the other moved up. I couldn't understand why they were so cautious, after all I was only one man, and it sounded like there was three or more of them.

My mind was racing, it was three in the morning and the

streets were deserted, except for me, and the three or four who were stalking me.

"Don't get caught in a spot where they can surround you, look for a place where you can defend yourself," I said to myself, busily looking for that right spot.

But where, there ... over there ... was that my best bet, a high wall with room to maneuver, yes ... If I can only get there.

I ran, only to pull up short, a shadow elongated itself across the wall. Damn, they beat me to it. "Where next?" I said again to myself, "Just keep looking and hope you get to the next vantage point before they do."

The persistent clatter of their footfalls, caution thrown to the winds echoed from the sides of the buildings. Those buildings, with all those people, but not one of them prepared to help. And why should they, they have to live here in this environment.

Still I thought of calling out but I knew it would be useless, especially in this neighborhood ... their neighborhood. I also did not want to give them any more information about me, like how scared I really was. Calling for help would be a dead give-a-way.

It was then I caught sight of one of them, he was trying to blend into a darkened doorway but was a fraction too slow. The sleazy bastard was grinning, he also had a long shiny object in one hand.

He stood or rather he slithered along, swinging that object in the doorway. My guess was he was waiting for my next move.

I didn't make one, I stood stock still in the middle of the street, waiting. Waiting to see how many there would be and where they were. A movement to my right caught my eye and without turning my head I saw two more of them. Both were also carrying some sort of shiny object in their hands.

Well, so far there were three of them and my instincts told me that wasn't all. By the footsteps there had to be at least five of them, and slowly from my left the other two emerged from an alley.

So, there it was … five to one … not really my preference … but then again nobody consulted me in the first place, now did they?

My first instinct was to run.. that was funny.. Where? They almost had me surrounded and in a second they would be on me if I decided to run. No running was not the answer, not yet.

I was wondering where the first attack would come from, I didn't expect them to wait, but they did. All of them just stood there, doing nothing. I turned my head and tried to pick out the leader but none of them looked the part.

Not one of them even assumed the attitude naturally associated with a leader. It puzzled me. That's a strange feeling, in the middle of being scared witless to also be puzzled … Christ, I wasn't prepared for that.

Nor was I prepared for what happened next. As I was trying to pick out a leader, someone, and I thank whoever it was, dumped a pail full of hot water on the sleazy one in the doorway. It caused him to drop his weapon and turn his back on me. Cursing and yelling up at the window he forgot about me long enough for me to race up the sidewalk and grab the thing he dropped. It was a length of pipe, with one end taped to form a handle, it was obviously his personal plaything.

Moving back out to the middle of the street I stood, with the pipe at the ready. I silently thanked the person who either wittingly or unwittingly gave me my first little edge. And little it was, because now the others started moving in, their weapons shining in the moonlight.

They were armed with two steel pipes that looked similar to the one I was holding, two lengths of chains doubled around their hands and lastly a long, really long gleaming shaft of steel ... a switchblade.

They all moved silently now, slowly circling me, inching closer, a side step, a feint, moving closer all the time. Chains swinging, pipes slapped against palms, closer now but not too close. What were they waiting for? The time seemed to stand still, my breath was low and a trickle of sweat rolled down my back. I was scared, but not as much as I thought I'd be. The waiting was getting unbearable, why didn't they make their move? I felt like shouting out for them to come and get me, wanting to get it over with once and for all. And still they waited ...

All of a sudden I knew why, I also knew why I couldn't pick out a leader. He had given his orders and was sitting back, waiting.. waiting to see what I was going to do. Sizing me up, laying back in the shadows. Well, I was going to draw him out somehow. I was going to make him show himself and make some sort of move. After all I didn't have all night ... what a laugh ... I didn't have all night!! I might not have a night after this was all done.

"Okay you creeps, let's go, not one of you has the brains you were born with. Which one of you wants to be first. Come on ... who wants to get wasted first or don't you ever think for yourselves," I said it slowly and calmly looking into the yellowish eyes of the one whose pipe I was swinging, hoping it would either goad him onto action or bring out their leader. Nothing ... not even a whisper. I had to admit it to myself, he was a cool customer.

"Before I bury this thing in your skull, you either move or make a noise, creep," I said with more courage than I really had.

Nobody made a move, nobody made a sound. I began to back up, trying to get some protection for my back. I backed up until I could feel the chassis of a car behind me. Better a car behind me than one of them, I thought.

They still hovered around, not making a sound, just threatening, it was weird ... I wondered, would he turn them loose and why was he waiting so long. The longer he waited though the more room I could maneuver in, I thought.

They were fanned out in front of me now and I could count the scars and pimples on their faces. The sweat on their faces gave me a clue as to what they were feeling and I could see fear also in their eyes. Strange, they had the edge and still they were scared. But not as much as I.

Suddenly I was grabbed from behind. An iron grip held me against the body of the car. I pulled away once and felt the point of a knife against my back.

"Make another move like that mister, and you are dead. Drop the pipe ... now!!"

I did as I was told and sleazy moved in and picked up his pipe. They had worked me perfectly, just where they wanted me. I had played right into their hands.

I was still being held firmly from behind, my mind tried to fathom just what I could do and what they really wanted from me. Anytime they wanted they could have taken my wallet and beaten me senseless, but still they held back. Why?

From behind me the voice spoke again, "You got a lotta guts mister. You talk big. I like that, shows you're not just another punk. Too bad you gotta get messed up. Wallet, rings and all your loose change on the hood. When I let you go, no funny or stupid moves or I bury this knife in your back."

Sleazy and his friends grinned, I could feel the bile rising in my throat. I unclasped my watch and slid it off my hand, my ring was next and as I was about to reach for my wallet I heard the car door open on the other side.

I tensed my hand and hit sleazy across the bridge of his nose with a karate chop that sent him sprawling to the gutter, both hands to his face to try stopping the blood from his broken and mangled nose. Just as quickly the others moved in. I ducked down and picked up the pipe sleazy had dropped and swung it at ankle level.

I caught one of them full on the outer part of his ankle, but before I could shift position two of them were on me. I felt pain in my left shoulder and glanced upward just in time to see a chain coming down on me again. I moved just in time to avoid it but caught a kick in the stomach for my trouble.

The leader was coming around the other side of the car and was about to join in when I hit one of them with the pipe on the side of his head. He staggered back as blood spurted out of his ear. The leader pushed him aside as three of them pulled me up and pushed me against the side of the car. A knife flashed in the bright moonlight. I tried to sidestep, the knife caught me just below the ribcage on my right side, but I managed to swing the pipe. I caught the hand that held the knife and it flew to the street and clattered away.

Someone grabbed my hair from behind and pulled me back while another started to work on my face. I reached out ... somewhere in my memory was a karate training bulletin ... "If you have the need ... grab it."

I did, I grabbed some ones ear and pulled. I heard a high

pitched wailing scream. As suddenly as it started, the pummeling and slashing stopped. I slumped against the car.

"You son of a bitch, I should have killed you right off the bat."

Through my puffed up, bloody eyes I saw the leader raise a pipe, I also saw his left ear dangling and bloody. His eyes were full of pain and fear. He threw the pipe at me and turned and ran, his gang of toughs limping after him.

The pipe miraculously missed me and clattered to the sidewalk harmlessly.

I had won … oh yeah … I had won. I slumped once more, fighting off the pain and nausea and tried not to pass out.

In the distance I heard the sirens, and grinning for the first time in what seemed a very long time I gave my final effort. I pulled myself up and leaned against the car in a devil may care pose and waited for my protectors in blue …

The End

End Of The Rainbow

There I was on my way to work, it was about 7:30 A.M. in the morning, and as usual the traffic was on the heavy side. The road was a little slick from an early morning shower and up ahead I could see a rainbow stretched across the sky. My eyes rested on the colors for just a moment and then went back to the traffic in front of me . It seemed the entire sky was alight with color and all of a sudden, and it seemed to take only an instant. One minute I was in traffic and the next I was bathed in those colors. Blues, yellows, greens and pink, they invaded every pore of my body and seemed to seep into and behind my eyes. I could swear that I could taste different color tinges on the tip of my tongue .

There was no sound inside the car, even though I had the radio on with music playing, I heard the traffic noises but they seemed very far away. I wondered if I had fallen asleep at the wheel momentarily, but I couldn't have, I saw all the cars around me and I saw people in the street all moving naturally along, and I was not out of control, on the contrary, but it also seemed that I was floating along on the colors.

The interior of the car was bathed in a combination of colors that splashed across the seats and the windshield, luminescent colors of blue, gold, violet and pink. The backs of my hands seemed to vibrate with a bluish purple haze as I grasped the steering wheel, and then they turned yellowish white with sparkles glinting off my fingernails. I know I should have been confused but it was all so peaceful that I could not work up a good case of nervousness or even fear. It was all I could do to keep up with the changing color scheme.

From somewhere I heard the sound of rushing wind, not a harsh sound, but some kind of cool and refreshing breeze, like right off the ocean after the rain. It added to the feeling of peace as it swirled the colors around the inside of the car.

So far I hadn't looked outside the car for a while and when I did I noticed that no one else had been effected the same way that I had, as a matter of fact when I took a longer look my heart did flip flops. I was well above the traffic and I was floating inside the bands of color, they were carrying me over all the traffic . The colors were changing so fast my eyes couldn't keep up with them. I was in the middle of the rainbow, I mean,pot of gold, and all that stuff.

The bands of color seemed to go on for miles, over the

tops of tall buildings, over the ocean, and I was headed in that direction. I had been transported by the rainbow and to tell the truth I really didn't care. My mind seemed to be held in a state of suspension, nothing mattered to me just as long as I could stay in that rainbow.

It was just about then that I heard voices, coming from all around me. Not in any language that I could recognize, but somehow they went into my head and I understood them. They seemed to tell me not to be afraid and I wasn't, since the start I hadn't been afraid. I'm not a person who believes in magic or extra-terrestrials, but I knew what they wanted from me and I was happy to comply.

They were saying, "Keep going, we'll take care of you, nothing will harm you." I trusted them, from what reasoning this came from I haven't the slightest idea, but I know I trusted them.

I don't know how long I had been with them or how long I would be staying with them, but I felt a kind of peacefulness just being there. I drifted along on the rainbow highway until it sloped downward to a rocky place unknown to me and my car came to a slow smooth stop. I looked around and it seemed to be calm all around me. I opened my door and stepped out into a sort of indentation in the ground. There was no one around but I still heard the voices, sometimes loud and sometimes softer, but they were still with me.

I could see colors flashing on and off, red white and blue,

they seemed to be synchronized, red white and blue, constantly flashing different from the other colors that I had gotten used to.

I heard a voice coming from behind me and I thought at last I'll be able to talk to them, and see them finally.

"Hey, buddy," I heard, "Are you ok, what are you doing out here, is everything alright?"

I turned and standing a few feet from me was a rather large man, all in blue, with a badge on his chest, yep, he was a policeman and the flashing lights I had seen were from his cruiser.

Slowly, I came to realize that I had driven onto the shoulder of the road and was standing outside of my car staring into the sky at the rainbow.

"Yes," I said to the officer, " I guess I just wanted to enjoy the colors of the rainbow before they disappeared, so I pulled over to be out of the traffic, I'm alright officer. Thank you for your concern,"

"Well, just be careful getting back on the highway, " he said," and have a nice day."

"I will and thanks again," I replied.

What he didn't know, was that I had already had the nicest day I have ever had, and I thanked the rainbow for it.

The End.

Printed in the United States
by Baker & Taylor Publisher Services